THE BRIDGE

DEATH ON THE HOMEFRONT

WAYNE W. ARNTSON

To order additional copies of this book, contact:
Bookwhip
1-855-339-3589
https://www.bookwhip.com

DEDICATION

This book is dedicated to the women in my life
who made it possible:

Margaret, Kim, and Sheri

With a special note of thanks to Dave

CHAPTER 1

U.S. Fortresses Pound Naples

—Duluth News Tribune, Summer, 1943

The foghorn moaned across shrouded Lake Superior and echoed off the rocky hills of Duluth, a sound Dave imagined coming from a wounded, bull elephant. My feelings exactly, he thought.

He shivered. Maybe from the melancholy sound. Maybe from the cold, foggy air. Maybe from his fear of their morning mission. He glanced at his partner, Jake, hoping his shudder had gone unnoticed. Jake never broke stride, and the two continued toward the source of the sound and the lift bridge.

Light traffic, two cars and a bus, moved slowly through the haze, headlights forming twin cones of light in the fog. Car traffic was always light, of course, what with gas and tire rationing. Most people rode the bus.

"How far did you say the bridge went up?" asked Dave.

"It's over a hundred feet," Jake replied, "but that don't make no difference, Aune. Once you're up over fifty feet, it don't matter how much farther you fall. You're dead."

What the hell am I doing here? Dave thought. He didn't like heights and that bridge was going to be slippery. Could he hang on? But he promised Jake he'd do it and no man breaks his promise.

"Remember," said Jake, "get your legs up over the top of that beam as soon as you can. Then wiggle your body up. You can't hang on all that time with just your arms. We may be up there for some time, you know."

Dave knew. Duluth was a busy harbor during World War II—most of the iron ore for the country came through the port. The bridge that connected their homes on Park Point with downtown Duluth could be up for over two hours if the boat traffic was heavy. He sighed to himself.

"And lock your hands on the other side of the beam," Jake advised. "Those steel babies will be so cold and slippery from this fog you'll never hang on unless you lock your hands."

Lock your hands. Right. Even in the cold of the morning fog Dave could feel his hands sweating. Even if I lock them they may slide apart.

Dave reviewed again how he had gotten into this adventure. He and Jake shared their adventures, including taking excursions in their little "boat." Jake couldn't swim and feared water, but, as he said, "A man's got to do some things even if he's scared. It shows you're a man, Aune!" Dave disliked heights so he needed to overcome his fear and prove his manhood. A secret trip on the bridge would do it.

But couldn't they do it on a sunny day?

Jake read Dave's thoughts. "We could wait for better weather, Aune, but then we'd probably get spotted and chased away. Nope, it's a perfect day to ride that monster." As he spoke, the specter of the bridge superstructure revealed itself through the gloom. They neared their destination.

An earlier scouting expedition had convinced the two that the downtown side of the bridge was the best approach. They started across the span and the sound of their footfalls changed to hollow, spooky warnings. Dave slowed and peered over the railing.

"C'mon, Aune, we've got to get across this thing before some ship starts comin' in and ruins our chance to get in position."

The foghorn bellowed again, painfully loud.

Following Jake's lead, Dave broke into a trot and the two crossed the four-hundred-foot span in short order. Running down the opposite side, Dave reached the bottom, turned right, and headed toward the pier.

The concrete piers under the bridge curl along the shore on the harbor side and extend over a thousand feet into Lake Superior on the other. A lighthouse and a foghorn punctuate the ends on the lake side. Walking directly under the bridge, they climbed over the inner wall and stationed themselves below the support beams that form an X between the two sides of the bridge. The support beams, unlike the massive side beams, are smaller, and have space above them, room enough for an uninvited passenger to lie on top.

"Don't grab the beam until she's ready to go up or somebody will spot us and chase us out of here," said Jake.

"There's nobody around and the operator can't possibly see us," Dave replied. The operator, the man who ran the bridge, was stationed in a little cabin at the middle of the span and twenty feet above the traffic.

"Yeah, but somebody could show up any minute, and we don't want to take a chance. Old man Brastad could stroll by in his little helmet."

"'The Bastard' is up at his store by now, counting his money," Dave said, thinking to himself that it wouldn't be the worst thing to happen if they did get noticed.

Crouching below the beam, Dave could feel the cold seeping into his bones and his stomach knotting. The only noise was the sorrowful foghorn and the occasional vehicle humming across the slatted steel of the bridge. They had to wait. *Wish I had my watch.*

Time crept by as the boys sat motionless, not wanting to reveal their positions to any passerby. Then, in the distance, a ship blew its deep-throated whistle: Once, twice, and a third time. It was the signal.

Moments later the bridge answered with three blasts of its own, a higher-pitched sound unmistakable to trained ears. The ship asked permission and the bridge said yes. In minutes the ascent would start.

Dave and Jake looked at each other, stood up and reached for the under beams. *Lock your hands,* Dave recalled, and he pulled his body up and tried to get his legs over the beam. The first attempt was unsuccessful as his foot slid off the wet metal. He tried a second time and the bridge started moving upward.

Dave found himself dangling from the underside of the bridge, holding on with his locked hands, debating what to do. He could drop from his position to the ground and abort the adventure, or he could cling to the beam and try again to get his legs over the top. He hesitated and time decided his fate—he was thirty feet up and rising, too late to drop.

"Get your legs up!" he could hear Jake yelling at him

Unnecessary advice. Dave was doing his best to get his body over the top. The bridge continued its ascent.

With a final, desperate lunge Dave hooked his right leg over the beam, and slowly worked his body up. Success! He was on top of the beam, clinging with locked hands—and seriously frightened.

He glanced at Jake. His partner was in the same position. Looking the opposite way, he spotted the hazy outline of an ore boat heading directly toward the bridge. The huge ship moved silently, ghost-like, into the channel and passed under the bridge. There was the bow, slicing through the waves. Then the elongated, ore-holding midsection. Finally the stern, its smokestack and superstructure reaching upward just below the elevated span. For a moment, Dave forgot his fear and watched in awe as the huge vessel slipped through the narrow passageway.

Once the ship was safely in the harbor, its whistle sounded again, this time two blasts. Dave cringed as the bridge answered with two honks of its own. God, that's loud! he thought, and clung ever tighter to the beam.

Why aren't we moving back down? Dave thought. Seconds later the answer came in the way of three blasts from another ore boat. The bridge answered and remained elevated. Dave's arms began to cramp.

The second ship crept through the channel as fatigue plagued him. He wondered how Jake was holding up. Finally, the vessel made the harbor and gave its two blasts. The bridge answered and, after an interminable amount of time, began its descent. Dave relaxed slightly. A mistake.

His left leg slipped from its position and dragged his right leg and eventually his whole torso off the top of his support. Dave clung to the beam, dangling in the air like a hooked trout, his locked hands the only thing between him and eternity. *I have to hang on. I have to hang on,* he thought. But he could feel his wet hands slowly slipping apart.

"Hold on!" Jake yelled.

Dave tried to get his right leg back up over the beam, but the long period of clinging to the steel had taken its toll. His muscles failed to respond. He squinted his eyes shut to concentrate on his hands. *Hang on! Hang on!*

Finally, he could take no more—his hands separated and he slipped from the bridge to his eternal fate…

* * *

Dave fell three feet onto the grass where he had started. The bridge settled into its base, and Jake rushed over to check on the health of his friend.

"Are you OK, buddy?"

Dave lay stunned and speechless as the foghorn grumbled in the background. He was still alive! Nothing was broken!

He sat up and smiled. "Wait until I tell Mary Ann!"

CHAPTER 2

Beef ration points boosted—scarcity cited

Duluth News-Tribune, Summer, 1943

The two young adventurers stood, stretched their cramped bodies, then stared at each other in amazement. Dave was the first to speak.

"Wow!"

"I told you it would be worth it," Jake said, smiling.

"I thought I was a goner for a while; my hands just wouldn't hold anymore."

"I knew you'd make it."

Dave looked up at the monstrous structure and slowly began to comprehend what they had done. *He could be dead now.* A feeling of delayed fear crept into his body and his legs began to tremble.

"Scared, DA?" asked Jake. He often called his pal "DA" saying that Dave was no name for a strong male.

"Naw. Legs just worn out from trying to get back up on that beam."

Jake glanced toward the bridge and nodded his head. "Let's get out of here. My dad wants me to help him today and I gotta be home in the next half hour."

At that news, Dave stopped breathing and silently stared after his friend striding toward the sidewalk. So, he's working for his dad again. Not good news. The alcoholic "Buck" Anderson had been known to get mean when he drank. Jake sometimes emerged from those sessions with bruises. Dave blinked himself back to reality, his elation of a minute ago subdued. He hurried to catch his pal, but neither one said another word on the subject.

The two boys clattered over the bridge and back toward their homes. One block before reaching Scotty O'Doul's place they turned across a vacant lot and headed toward the beach. Scotty would be sitting on his front porch at this hour and they had been avoiding him since that winter-storm/car incident.

The lake breeze picked up and began to disperse the early fog. Gulls circled noisily overhead, squawking for a handout, and the heavy overcast began to yield to a persistent sun. Some minutes later they neared the Anderson house and Jake turned toward his home.

"See ya later, DA. Great morning!"

"See you, Jake. Be careful."

Dave watched his friend disappear behind the sand dune at the top of the beach then continued on toward his own house.

"I'm home!" he shouted, as the screen door banged behind him.

"In the other room!" his mother yelled back.

Dave strolled back to his mother's bedroom and found her sitting on the bed surrounded by scraps of old cloth: sheets, towels, underwear, tablecloths—a potpourri of colors and textures. His eyebrows elevated in bewilderment.

"We have no use for these things anymore so some of us are going to sew them into quilts for the refugees. Don't you think they'll look nice?" She was a patriotic soul always doing something for "the war effort" or "our boys," the GIs. "We're going to meet at Mrs. Carlson's place as soon as we get ready. Do you want me to make you something to eat before I go?"

"No, I'm fine Ma. I'm going to pack a lunch and go up to the bridge and watch a few ships."

"O.K., dear, have fun."

Dave walked to the kitchen, found a can of sardines in the cupboard, and pulled a loaf of bread from the shelf. He partially opened the sardine can with the attached key, drained the excess oil into the sink, and then removed the top entirely. Next, he got the breadboard and knife and sliced off two slabs. Reaching into the sardine can with a fork, he removed one little fish, and popped it into his mouth. Delicious! The rest of the sardines he put atop one slice of bread and covered them with the other slice. He wrapped the delicacy in a piece of wax paper, jammed it into his jacket pocket, and prepared to leave. Why the big fuss over making meals? It was a snap.

"See you later, Ma!"

"Bye, dear. Be careful."

Dave stepped outside and unexpected, bright sunshine caused him to shade his eyes. The day was quite magnificent with a gentle lake breeze and warming temperatures. Turning toward the beach, he retraced his earlier steps and headed toward the bridge, again avoiding O'Doul's house.

In a matter of fifteen minutes Dave was back at the bridge. As he started across, he saw her: Mary Ann, standing on the far pier in a light blue dress, looking out at the lake with her long blonde hair waving in the breeze and reflecting the best parts of the sunshine. He paused for a moment and drew in a deep breath. Someday I'm going to find a girl like that who's my age.

Dave ran the rest of way across the bridge and down onto the pier.

"Dave! Nice to see you! Isn't this a gorgeous day!"

"Hi, Mary Ann. Yup, it's pretty nice." She looked even lovelier close up.

"Where's Jake?"

"He had to go work for his dad."

She blinked and her countenance darkened. "Oh, dear. I hope everything goes all right." She was familiar with the bad temper of Buck Anderson.

Not wanting to get into that discussion, Dave changed the subject and inquired, "How are things at *Piggly Wiggly?*"

"About normal, I guess. Poor old Mrs. Severson came in again today looking for a big jar of beans. It's fourteen cents and twelve points. She got her ration book out but only had three five-point stamps and we can't give change so she was going to lose three points. We finally got that explained to her and she decided to go ahead and lose the three points, but then she couldn't understand why she had to pay fourteen cents, too!"

"Did she finally get her beans?"

"Yes, she did. But it's no wonder she's confused. They keep changing the point requirements; they go up because there's a 'scarcity' or they go down because of a 'plentiful crop.' Poor lady. And she's not the only one. The rumor is that we'll be able to give ration-point change when they issue the new books in October. I hope so. Poor lady."

Dave listened with half an ear. She's probably the nicest nineteen-year-old girl in the city, he thought. His eyes caught the gold airplane on a chain that Mary Ann constantly wore around her neck. A gift from her fiancée in the Army Air Corps, the pendant had been specially made in the shape of the twin-fuselaged P-38, the hottest new plane in the U.S. arsenal. Dave remembered the first time he and Jake saw the necklace just a month earlier. They were both fascinated and afterward Dave asked Jake how he liked the airplane and Jake replied he was more interested in the landing field. They both laughed briefly then became embarrassed: You don't say such things about a nice girl like Mary Ann.

"What do you hear from Dean?"

"He's awfully busy but enjoys the training. He still hopes to fly a P-38. Oh, and he said to tell you and Jake hello. He was quite impressed with you two last month." She paused, smiled, and looked admiringly at her young friend.

"Dave, I think you get taller every time I see you! My gosh, when I first baby sat you a few years ago, you were just a little kid running around in short pants!"

He remembered very well. And he remembered the little talk the two of them had a couple years ago, about different kinds of love and finding a girl his age and how they would be good friends forever. She was a good friend. An adult who talked to him as an equal—but whose compliments made him uneasy. He stared at his feet then out at the water and suddenly didn't know what to do with his hands. Mary Ann noted his uncomfortable demeanor and moved to another topic.

"What did you do this morning?

"Jake and I rode the bridge."

"You what?!"

Mary Ann's comments and her obvious dismay were interrupted by a sudden blare from the bridge as it answered an incoming ship. Dave, surprised by her reaction, was almost sorry when the three, teeth-rattling blasts came to an end.

"You might have been killed!"

"Nah, it went real smooth. Great view from up there."

"Dave, Dave, Dave, I never thought you two would really do it. I'm glad I didn't know ahead of time." She shook her head and glanced out at the incoming ore boat. Then, while her hackles were still raised, she broached another topic Dave liked to avoid. "Have you talked to Mr. O'Doul yet?"

"No, not yet. I guess I'll have to stop in to see him soon."

"It wasn't your fault, you know. I'm sure he doesn't blame you two."

"Maybe I'll stop by on the way home." Dave stared at the passing ship and considered the possibility. He really should have Jake with him.

"I've got to run back to work," Mary Ann said. "Take care of yourself and say hi to Jake."

Dave watched as she turned, ascended the steps to the walkway, and headed back toward downtown.

He didn't know it would be the last time he would see her.

CHAPTER 3

Violent Storm Hits Area—Park Point Cut Off

Duluth News-Tribune, March, 1943

Dave pulled the squashed sandwich from his pocket and peeled back the wax paper. The smell of sardines filled the air as he took his first bite and stared out at the big water. What a glorious day! He had just talked to his favorite girl, he had conquered the big bridge, and the food was terrific. He wolfed down another bite of the delicacy then held the remaining lunch in front of him and admired his masterpiece. From nowhere, a large gull flashed over his head, swooped low, and speared the remains of the sardine sandwich from his hand.

"You son of a… !" He lunged belatedly at the bird and then watched in anger as the big, white thief swooped out over the canal, parts of the booty plopping into the water where they were scooped up by other members of the flock. Damn!

Pausing for a few seconds, he regained his composure. No use getting excited over a little piece of sandwich, he thought. Then he turned, walked up the steps to a water fountain, quenched his thirst, and started back toward home.

As his hollow footsteps marked his trail across the bridge, Dave began to think of Mary Ann's advice: Go talk to Mr. O'Doul. That's probably a good idea, he thought; we've been avoiding him long enough. After all, it wasn't his fault or Jake's fault or Birdy's fault either. They just followed orders. And if it hadn't been for the big snowstorm, the whole incident might never have occurred… .

* * *

It was the middle of March that year when the blizzard struck. Dave heard from the old-timers how "nor'easters" blow in off the lake and broadside the Point with enormous amounts of snow. Maybe, he thought, those are just fogey stories meant to impress young listeners. While it was true that he saw huge waves crash in on the beach during summer thunderstorms, he had yet to witness a big, winter whiteout.

Monday morning dawned slate-gray and grew progressively darker as the hours went by. By noon, even sitting by the window, Dave needed a lamp to read, and his mother commented on the threatening day. After lunch, the wind picked up and a few flurries swirled around the house. By suppertime, when Dave's father Carl arrived home, travel was treacherous.

"It's getting nasty out there!" he said, stomping his feet to remove the snow. "Our bus slipped all over the road; hope I can get to work tomorrow."

Tena, Dave's mother, said nothing but continued her preparation of their meal, making kitchen noises with pots and pans. The wind howled around their house and Dave felt glad to be snug inside.

Early the next morning he awoke and walked barefoot out to the living room of their small home. Only the tops of the windows were not masked by drifts and snow continued to fall heavily. The wind, now muffled by snow banks, continued its onslaught. Carl sat in the kitchen sipping coffee and pondering how to get to work.

The blizzard continued for most of the day. Carl never did get to work. In the late afternoon when the flurries diminished, Dave and his dad forced the front door open at the top. Dave squeezed through the small opening carrying a small ash shovel and proceeded to dig around the door until it could be opened. Carl joined his son outside and the two of them surveyed the polar landscape still being buffeted by gale-force winds.

It was either a wonderland or a disaster.

The howling wind blew over the beach, up the gradual slope, and down the backside where it swirled and deposited massive quantities of snow on homes and completely blocked the one street that runs the length of the island. The two saw no person, no animal, no machine and the only sound was the wailing nor'easter.

"Let's go back in and see what the radio has to say," said Carl. They stepped inside, shivering with cold and apprehension, grateful to get out of the wind.

For a day the Aunes remained inside and amused themselves by playing *Monopoly* and listening to the radio. On the second day, Carl, ever the faithful employee, walked over the drifts and across the bridge to catch a ride to work. On that same day, the bus company managed to dig a path from the Point side of the bridge down to the beach where winds had blown the shoreline relatively free of snow. Buses traveled the lakeside route and provided rides to downtown Duluth for the stranded Pointers who were unable to walk that far.

Dave explored the snow-clad neighborhood. The depth of the snow was incredible—he walked atop the hard-packed drifts over the street and reached *down* to touch the tops of utility poles. Cars had disappeared under the white blanket and owners jabbed hastily-constructed signs in the drifts, each marking a spot where a vehicle was buried.

It wasn't until a week after the storm that the street was opened. Traffic resumed and gradually, over the next month, the snow melted, automobiles were reunited with their owners, and activities returned to normal.

Two weeks after the storm, Jake and Dave walked along the street looking at the blizzard-inflicted damage. Tree branches cluttered the landscape; buildings, collapsed from the burden of all the precipitation, sat waiting for repair.

"I guess this is what the old-timers were talking about," said Davey. Then he paused, looked down the street, and grabbed Jake's shoulder. "Listen. Is that Birdy?"

In the distance they heard a familiar voice singing, "*Super Suds, Super Suds* lots more suds with *Super Su-u-uds.* Richer, longer lasting too, it's the suds with super do-oo-oo." It had to be Birdy.

Birdy Gunderson, a year younger than Dave, built like a stork and noted for his peculiarities kept his schoolmates entertained. His real name was Bertram, his family called him "Berty," and, because of his constant singing and whistling, his classmates dubbed him "Birdy." He was friendly to everyone, nobody's good friend, and addicted to the radio. His favorite songs were commercials.

"Hi, guys," said Birdy, emerging from some brush. "What are you doing?"

"Just lookin' at the damage," Jake replied.

"Me too," said Birdy, and with no further comment, began to whistle the *Rinso-White* song which purportedly contained a quail whistle, although nobody Dave knew had ever heard a quail. Jake and Dave stared at each other momentarily, smiled, and continued their walk with Birdy tagging along, whistling and oblivious to the surroundings.

A voice caught their attention. "Hey, boys, come on up here. I got a business proposition for you." Scotty O'Doul stood on his porch waving for the three to come up.

"Wonder what it is this time?" Jake mumbled.

"Maybe he wants us to dig out that basement he's always talking about," said Dave. The three walked toward the O'Doul house.

"Fer crissake," Scotty said to the three when they reached his porch, "ain't that a mess!" He gestured toward the lone box elder tree in the center of his lawn. "Most of the branches broke off and I had to hire old Charlie Bracken to saw them up and haul them away. And the tree will probably die, too, fer crissake!" The three boys stood mutely, waiting for the proposition.

"The thing is, I can't get my Ford started and I need your help."

Dave pondered that comment. Scotty had a '34 *Ford* stored in his back yard; he never drove it but he would start it occasionally just to "make sure it's ready in case of emergency." What could the three of them do to help?

"The weather has been too cold to get that baby going," Scotty continued, "so I have to warm up the engine. That's where you three come in."

Dave and Jake looked at each other, but neither knew yet how they could help. Meanwhile, Birdy whistled quietly to himself and gazed at some distant object only he could see.

"I built a little fire out back but don't have enough power to push my baby over it. C'mon, I'll show you."

The four of them walked around back where Scotty's car sat, apparently no worse for wear from the storm. Six feet in front of car a small bonfire smoked, stoked with green boughs, flotsam from the storm. One small flame flickered in the damp fuel and Jake suggested that not much heat was being given off.

"She's just perfect!" said Scotty, "Don't want to burn up the car, just heat the engine.

"Here's where you guys come in. I'll give each of you twenty-five cents if you help me push this baby over the fire. What do you say?!"

Birdy snapped out of his reverie: "You betcha!"

The other two felt a little more reluctant. They knew Scotty quite well. He was self-described as "half Welch, half Irish, and full of Scotch!" His schemes often fell on the far side of goofy. But, they reasoned, what could go wrong? The die was cast.

The three boys positioned themselves behind the car while Scotty stood off to the side. "She'll be a little tough to move, but it's slightly downhill and you guys are strong. I'll tell you when to stop. Ready?"

The pushers nodded. "Go!" Scotty shouted.

At first push, nothing happened. Then slowly, reluctantly the old jalopy crept forward, apparently fearful of the smoking mass in front of it. The boys struggled, hands sliding off the slanted trunk, feet slipping on the muddied ground. "A little more, boys! That's it! Good! A little more! Hold her right there!"

The three stopped pushing, leaned against the cold *Ford*, and panted for breath.

"That's perfect," said Scotty. "See, the smoke is coming from just under the engine. In a few minutes I'll have that baby purring like a new Caddy."

The four of them watched as smoke curled up and around the engine compartment. Dave wondered when they'd get their money. Birdy began humming the *Cream of Wheat* commercial. Scotty stood with arms folded, smiling at his vehicle. Jake bent down and peered under the car at the smudge-pot fire.

"There's a little more fire under there now, Mr. O'Doul," Jake said.

"Good," Scotty said, "she'll warm up faster then."

Jake continued his watch. "You better look at this, Mr. O'Doul. Those flames are getting higher!"

Scotty took a few steps toward the car, knelt down, peeked under the running board, and jumped back with agility seldom seen by men his age. "Fer crissake, some of the oil under there is burning! We got to push her back!"

He motioned the boys to the front of the car and exhorted them to push. "Fer crissake, push!"

The three tried to push but made no headway; after all, it was slightly uphill.

The fumes grew heavier and the boys, coughing, choking, and gasping for breath, staggered back from the car.

"Fer crissake," said Scotty, "run down to the fire department and send them up here!" Birdy, fast as a whippet, took off on the fly toward the Park Point fire hall only two blocks away. Scotty, Dave, and Jake stepped back and watched helplessly as the flames began licking their way around the engine compartment. Moments later, light could be seen coming from the interior of the car and the upholstery burst into fire.

When the fire department arrived, the old *Ford* was in full flame. They could do nothing but watch and make sure no surroundings caught on fire. Scotty seemed to be in a daze and the three boys watched in wonder.

"Let's get out of here," Jake whispered.

"Good idea," said Dave, and the three boys slowly backed up and eased their way from the scene.

"But we didn't get our quarters!" said Birdy.

* * *

Dave sighed to himself as he recalled the events. Yeah, I should stop and see Mr. O'Doul, he thought. Then he turned, cut across the vacant lot, and headed toward the beach. Maybe tomorrow.

CHAPTER 4

U.S. Builds 7200 Planes In May

Duluth News Tribune, Summer, 1943

Dave's brand-new, twin-tailed P-38 hummed along quietly as he scanned the jungle-clad island below. The plane, only a month old, contained the new, top-secret superheterodynamic accelerator. He could hardly wait to try it out on those Nips. They'd be in for a surprise! Dropping lower, he squinted through the bright sunshine, trying to locate any enemy activity amidst the palm trees.

Then he spotted them—but not below.

High above and to his rear, two Jap Zeroes screamed toward his twin tails, intent on destruction. In a few seconds they would be in range to blow him to kingdom come. Perfect, he thought. Wait'll they see this! He reached forward and pulled on his superheterodynamic accelerator.

The aircraft leaped forward, the incredible thrust squashing Dave back into his seat. With great effort he forced his right hand forward and pulled back on the stick. The plane shuddered from the strain but began to climb: twenty degrees, forty, sixty, eighty and finally straight up! Continuing on his inside loop, Dave was momentarily upside down and weightless. Then, with his engines screaming, he plummeted straight down, directly behind his two enemies. He imagined the astonishment on their faces. A few seconds more and he'd have them in his gun sights.

"Aune! Aune!"

Damn radio, he thought. I don't have time for that now.

"Aune! Aune!"

I'm busy right now! Call you back later! I've got a bead on one!

His trigger finger began to tighten.

"Aune! Aune! Wake up!"

The battle scene began to fade. His friend's face came into view.

"She's dead," said Jake.

"Who's dead? What are you talking about?" He propped myself up on one elbow and tried to emerge from the curtain of sleep. This was not a good way for his pal to wake him up.

"Mary Ann is dead!"

Dave sat up in bed, dazed, wondering if he was still asleep, if this was the start of a new dream. His best friend Jake stood over him with a look of bewilderment and shock. Jake, the coolest kid in the world who never got concerned over anything, was showing anguish. And what was this about Mary Ann? Our Mary Ann?

"Mary Ann who?" he asked.

"Mary Ann Pleason is dead! She was found murdered early this morning!" Jake sat on the bed and stared off into space.

There must be a mistake. Death was not uncommon in those days of World War II—fathers, older brothers, uncles were regularly reported as casualties—but somebody right there in Duluth? Somebody they knew so well? Somebody as nice as Mary Ann?

"Are you sure?"

Jake's extraordinary demeanor was as disturbing as the news. He squirmed as he sat and struggled with his voice. "Old man Fralik found her body this morning when he was going to his store. She'd been strangled! Just a block from her house!"

Fraliks owned the local grocery store on Park Point. Mary Ann's house was between the store and Fralik's. It made sense. Well, at least it was logical. Mr. Fralik did take that route every morning.

Wide awake by then, Dave jumped into his clothes, donned his tennies and the two of them bolted out the front door. Dave's mother yelled after them, "Don't you want some breakfast, Davey?"

"No, Ma, I'll get it later."

The two boys ran down the hill to the only street on Park Point. Instinctively they knew where they were going. Reaching the road, they tacitly turned left and headed toward Mary Ann's house. Several blocks later four police cars and a scattered crowd of gawking onlookers came into view. Two of the cars were parked at the Pleason house, the others were closer to the apparent scene of the crime, a small area, roped off and containing four men, heads bowed, apparently looking for any clues on that desecrated ground.

Jake and Dave pressed forward, getting as close to the ropes as possible. A man inside the restricted area wearing a brown suit and hat (a detective?) bent over and retrieved a small object from the ground. He looked at it carefully, then pulled a small bag from his pocket, carefully placed the entity in the bag and wrote something on the outside. Was it the clue to solve the murder? The two pals watched in awe.

In 1943 radio was big and most boys listened to a fair share of detective stories: *Gangbusters, True Detective Mysteries, The Shadow.* Jake and Dave knew, or at least thought they knew, how detectives worked and how they quickly solved crimes.

"There's something over here!" Jake yelled at a policeman, pointing at a spot on the ground inside the ropes. The policeman looked up, strolled to the area where Jake was pointing, bent over and picked up a small, light-colored object. Examining the prize briefly, the officer turned, walked to Jake, extended his arm with the object and said, "Here you are, son—thanks for your help." Jake held out an open hand and received the evidence: a white piece of quartz. Embarrassed, he stepped back.

The two boys slowly, cautiously, sadly moved toward the Pleason house. While still some distance away, they spotted Mr. and Mrs. Pleason step out of their front door accompanied by a uniformed policeman. Mrs. Pleason clung to her husband's shoulder and sobbed intermittently. Mr. Pleason explained something to the officer and the three of them disappeared back into the house.

It was all the boys could handle. Without saying a word, with bowed heads, they turned to leave and bumped head on into Mr. Brastad.

"What are you boys doing here?" he demanded. "You should be home staying out of the way of the police. They have enough to do without having to work around gawking spectators!"

The boys said nothing. They just stared at their old nemesis, turned to one side, and walked back home, stunned with sorrow, anger, and disbelief.

In the following days Duluth buzzed with the news of murder. Police cars frequented the Point, visiting the Pleason house and its neighbors. Rumors of an imminent arrest passed like wildfire along the narrow confines of the island, but nothing came of it.

Three days after the incident Mary Ann was buried. Neither Dave nor Jake attended the funeral, but grieved by themselves as they sat by the bay and threw rocks and sticks into the water. Little was said. Dave felt thankful to have a good friend who felt the same way.

CHAPTER 5

Coupon #17 for Shoes to Expire

Duluth News Tribune, Summer, 1943

The day glowed with an intense sun, cotton candy clouds broke the monotony of the sky, and a gentle lake-breeze prevented overheating. The lake itself, as still as it ever gets, produced tiny waves that flopped repeatedly with soft splashing sounds. Gulls soared above, occasionally breaking the quiet with raucous calls.

Dave stopped his stroll, selected a pebble from the nearest rock pile, and flung it at an over-friendly bird. Missed. I must have thrown at a million birds over the years, and never came close to one, he thought.

"Nice throw, Bob Feller!" said Jake.

Dave smiled momentarily and then resumed his funk. The two continued their slow walk. Finally, Jake burst the silence with a sentence he'd been storing for some time:

"It's been over two weeks now and the police don't seem to be getting anywhere so what are we going to do about it?"

Dave stared at his partner. What could they do?

"I heard they gave up on 'The Bachelor,' but I'll bet he did it," Jake continued. "I saw a police car at his house a few days ago, but the guy still goes to work every morning.

"Maybe they're just waiting for more evidence," Dave replied.

"Meanwhile 'The Bachelor' goes free, keeps bringin' girls to his house, and is still on the loose. Why isn't he in the Army, anyway? He's healthy as a horse."

Dave pondered the question. Why wasn't he in the service? He was the only young man left on the Point who wasn't sick or crippled. And he was quiet. Oh, he'd say hello, but that's all. Went to work in the morning and returned at night. Sometimes he'd bring a female visitor home and they'd take a boat ride in his little sloop.

"And where does he work? Maybe he just goes downtown and drinks all day. Maybe he's a Nazi spy, Mary Ann found him out, and he had to kill her." Jake persisted.

Dave selected a flat rock from a pile of lake-scoured pebbles and skipped it across the water. Once, twice, three times it bounced and then went into what they called the "blur," the end of a skipping-rock journey where the stone makes so many little skips they blend into one "blur" just before sinking.

"Maybe it was somebody else," said Dave, "maybe it was old man O'Doul, although he's usually a pretty good guy." He skipped another rock and got four skips before the blur.

"O'Doul wouldn't do it. He doesn't leave his house long enough. But if you want to suspect old goats, how about "The Bastard"? His wife died years ago, he lives alone and has nothin' to do but run that hardware store and hassle us kids. What a jerk!"

"He's a jerk, all right, but probably not a killer. He does help out with paper drives and metal drives, and he is a blackout warden."

"Yeah, right," said Jake. "Now he wears that goofy helmet that says 'WARDEN' on it. Where did he get that thing? And if he's such a patriot, why doesn't he scrap that big, ugly, metal toad from his yard? It's big enough to make a tank. You and me, Aune, have to scrap that toad for him!" Jake selected a rock, flung it, and watched it skip six times, the record of the day.

"How about old man Fralik?" asked Dave. "He found Mary Ann. Maybe he killed her and then just *said* he found her. It makes a nice alibi."

"I don't think so. I was in his store yesterday and he still looks shook up. The day after, he couldn't even talk to people."

"Don't you think he'd be shook up and not want to talk if he *was* guilty?"

"OK, OK you can talk about all the men on the Point if you want to, but I still think it was 'The Bachelor'." Jake fired another rock; it skipped just twice before drowning.

Dave stared at his partner for several seconds. "So what if it is 'The Bachelor'? What can we do about it?" He threw a pebble that bounced five times, one short of the record.

Jake's eyes lit up. He was waiting for that question. "First we have to get his name and find out what he does downtown every day. Why isn't he in the army? Stuff like that. Then we can start to build our case"

Dave considered his friend's remarks. That last line about "build our case" came right from some detective show, but maybe he was right. Furthermore, Dave also considered "The Bachelor" the prime suspect. And investigating was better than just sitting around while the police did nothing.

"When do we start?"

"Tomorrow. We follow him downtown and see where he goes and find out what he does. We'll have to be careful, of course, since we don't want to end up like poor Mary Ann."

The sound of her name tightened Dave's stomach and he knew then he was doing the right thing. "I'll meet you tomorrow morning at 7:00 in front of Bakers' house. That's far enough away so he won't get suspicious but close enough where we can keep an eye on him."

"Sounds good," said Jake.

Dave found an extra-thin flat rock. He side-armed it toward the water in a final attempt to break the daily record. The missile soared across the waves, slowly twisted in the air, and hit the water edge first, disappearing like a coin in a slot.

"Guess I'll never be a professional stone-skipper," said Dave.

The two turned and headed back home, their minds filled with tomorrow's mission.

CHAPTER 6

U.S. and Canada Will Be Producing 1 Plane Every 5 Minutes

Duluth News Tribune, Summer, 1943

The two boys shivered in the early morning chill as they stood waiting for the bus. Bakers' house, their predetermined meeting spot, sat one bus stop away from, and within easy sight of, the bachelor's little cottage. The bus was due in four minutes and still no sign of their quarry.

"Where the heck is he?" said Jake.

"He's still got a couple minutes," Dave replied.

"What do we do if he don't show up?"

"Just wait until tomorrow, I suppose."

The seconds ticked by. Jake shifted back and forth between left foot and right foot. "Cold out here!" he said.

In the distance they spotted the oncoming bus.

"He's going to miss his ride!" said Jake.

Dave was about to suggest a retreat when he spotted the familiar figure in the distance. "There he goes across the road!"

The two watched in silence as the bachelor, neatly dressed in suit and tie, trotted across the avenue and stood by the utility pole with the orange band painted around it, the symbol of a bus stop.

Dave looked at his partner and the two nodded. So far so good. The old bus halted in front of them, its front door folded open, and

Dave followed his partner aboard. They dropped their tokens into the glass fare-box and proceeded to the rear, picking the last double seat available.

One block later the bus stopped again. The nattily-dressed bachelor sprang aboard, greeted the driver with smile, dropped his token in the box, and took a seat near the front.

"He didn't see us," said Dave.

Jake didn't reply but instead stared intently at the bus driver. "Do you see who's driving this thing? It's Elmer Fudd!"

The driver, a middle-aged man too old for the draft, regularly drove the Park Point route. A friendly, courteous fellow with excellent driving skills, he had one fault: a speech impediment. Bus drivers were required to call out the names of approaching, major streets. The main drag in downtown Duluth is Superior Street. This driver called it "Supeweeow Stweet" which always invoked chortles with the boys and inevitably led to the "Elmer Fudd" nickname.

Dave looked carefully to the front; sure enough, it was "Elmer."

Jake leaned over to Dave and spoke in his best Elmer Fudd voice, "Do you suppose he knows anything about Mawy's case?"

Ordinarily, any mention of Mary and her death cast a melancholy mood through Dave. This time, however, in his overwrought frame of mind, the silly comment caused the tension to burst forth in a guffaw that echoed through the vehicle. All eyes glanced back, looking for the source of the noise. The driver checked his rear-view mirror. Dave and Jake stared at the floor and struggled to maintain self-control.

A moment later the only noise was the humming of the tires as they passed over the lift bridge. The boys regained their composure and two minutes later heard, "Supeeow Stweet!" For some reason, the comment was not funny in the least.

The bus slowed to stop at the intersection. The bachelor rose from his seat and stood by the front door. Dave and Jake walked to the back door. Stepping outside, the boys turned their backs to the emerging bachelor and looked the other way. The bachelor ignored them, walked across Lake Avenue, and briskly strode down Superior Street. Dave and Jake followed some distance back.

After a short walk, the bachelor turned and entered a nondescript, multi-storied building filled with windows. "What is that place?" asked Dave.

"Beats me. Looks like a place for doctors and lawyers."

Hurrying to the entrance, they stepped inside to a stark lobby. Their quarry was nowhere in sight. A large, glass-covered sign hanging on the wall identified the occupants of the building. Dave and Jake approached and began to read:

Arnevik, Grivna, & Parker, Attorneys at Law 306
Blasczyk, J. P., Dental Surgery 410
Crisler, Schilling, & Schmid, Attorneys at Law 828

. . . .

"My God," said Jake, "there must be hundreds of rooms here. How are we going to find our man?"

Dave nodded in agreement. "It looks like there's fourteen stories to this place and each one has quite a few rooms."

"We could ride up that elevator and take a glance at each floor," said Jake. "Or maybe we should hang around until noon—the guy has to eat."

"Why don't we come back tomorrow morning and get to this building before the bachelor does. Then we could see which floor he goes to and maybe even follow him right up there."

Jake was silent for a minute, then sighed and nodded agreement. "We sure as hell can't find him in this big barn just by strolling around. C'mon, I'll buy you a hot chocolate at *Bridgman's*." Dave nodded agreement, they walked outside, and the pair of detectives walked silently to the ice cream store.

By the end of their chocolate treat, the plans were in place: Take an earlier bus downtown tomorrow, get to the building ahead of the bachelor, and tail him to his destination.

Little was spoken on the ride back home. Elmer Fudd was not driving, few people rode the bus, and their anxiety of early morning slowly gave way to fatigue. Dave wondered what the morrow would bring. Could they locate the bachelor's destination? What if they got caught by the bachelor's gang? What kind of cover was the man using?

Jake pulled the bell-cord to tell the driver to stop, and the vehicle halted in front of the big Anderson house. Dave and Jake jumped off, reiterated their plan to meet early the next day, then separated and returned to their homes.

CHAPTER 7

Rubber Scrap Drive to Start Wednesday

Duluth News Tribune, Summer, 1943

The next morning dawned cool, foggy, and grey, a gloomy copy of the previous day. Dave arrived first at the bus stop, his stomach in a tight knot, then watched with some relief as his pal approached a minute later.

"Morning."

"Morning."

"Chilly this morning," said Jake.

"Sure is," replied Dave.

The two stared down the avenue, looking for a sign of their bus.

"Damn thing's never on time, Dave!" said Jake.

Dave studied his friend. *He called me by my first name. He's a little shook up, too. Good. It's not just me.*

Their transportation came into sight.

The old bus grumbled to a stop, the bi-fold doors opened, and Dave followed his pal aboard. "Elmer" was not driving.

On reaching Superior Street, the two hopped off the bus and were greeted by a blast from the nearby foghorn and the smell of *Arco Coffee* in the air. "Some day we ought to go down to that coffee plant and see how they cook it," Dave said. But not on this day; they crossed Lake Avenue and headed straight for the big, office building where the bachelor disappeared the day before.

Entering the structure, Dave felt the solemnity of the large vestibule. The room was polished, modern, and barren, with not even a potted plant to disrupt the cold atmosphere. Old men in dark suits and young women in skirts, blouses, and a variety of hats, burst through the entrance in a steady stream and moved swiftly to the elevators where they impatiently awaited their turns. The clickety-clack of footsteps on the stone floor echoed off the cave-like room, drowning out the few whispers between waiting workers.

Realizing they had half an hour to wait for their quarry (a long time to read signs on the walls and appear normal to passing workers), Dave spoke up. "I'll go outside and watch and let you know when he's approaching." Jake nodded agreement and Dave exited to the street.

He sniffed the air. I wonder if other cities smell like coffee? People hustled by, oblivious to his presence. Across the street, on the corner, the old man with the newsstand stood in his usual spot, proffering the passers-by with the latest news of the war. "Homadisson hurl," he mumbled softly. "Homadisson hurl." That phrase was mysterious to Dave for a long time until someone told him the man was selling the local edition of the newspaper: The home-edition *Herald*. "Homadisson hurl." The old guy dressed in his usual garb of dark trousers, dark tattered coat, and black-knit, woolen cap pulled down over his ears. His uniform never changed, summer or winter, hot or cold. A landmark of downtown Duluth. Could he have had something to do with Mary's death? Nah, I don't think so.

Dave turned his eyes down the block to watch for the bachelor and was surprised to see him approaching, sooner than expected.

Dave pivoted and walked back into the office building. Jake saw his buddy and knew their man was near. The two turned to the glass-covered frames on the wall next to the elevators and feigned intense interest in the names of the occupants listed.

The bachelor entered, strode across the foyer, and stopped in front of the elevator. When the doors opened, he stepped inside and clearly told the operator, "Twelve, please." Others crowded into the small car, each announcing their floor, the doors closed, and the two boys stared at each other. "Twelve." They knew the floor; now to see what was up there.

As quickly as possible, so as not to lose their man, the pursuers crowded onto the next available elevator and told the operator, "Twelve." The teen-aged operator looked at them with surprise but said nothing. It wasn't his job.

Eventually, (they stopped at almost every floor) the operator called out, "Twelve," the door opened, and the two stepped out into surprising surroundings.

Instead of seeing hallways and office doors, they found themselves in a small lobby. Two wooden doors led out of the lobby but both were marked with "Authorized Personnel Only." A counter occupied a third of the wall space, and behind the counter stood a lovely young lady, dressed to the nines, with raven hair arranged in the latest Hedy Lamarr style.

"Can I help you, boys?" she said.

Dave felt stunned for a moment then answered, "We just saw our neighbor come in here and wanted to say hello."

"Oh, you mean Aaron. Yes, he just came in, but I'm afraid you just missed him. He went inside and, as you can see, only authorized personnel are allowed in. Tell you what, though, I'll be seeing Mr. Seacrest at noon and I'll tell him hello for you. What are your names?"

"I'm Donald," said Dave.

"And I'm Gerald," lied Jake.

"OK, guys, I'll tell him you were here."

"Thank you, ma'am."

The two backed up to the elevator doors, watching Miss Hedy Lamarr all the way, then turned and pushed the down button. After what seemed a very long time, the doors opened and they stepped inside the elevator. Stoically they waited, saying nothing, until they reached the main floor. Stepping out, they walked quickly across the lobby and pushed their way to the sidewalk.

Once outside the office building their self-imposed silence quickly shattered as they turned down Superior Street:

"What kind of place is that?" Dave blurted out, eyes wide-open in wonderment.

"There wasn't a sign on the door and nothin' on the inside either!" said Jake, "and when you were outside, I checked over all those listings on the walls of the lobby, and, you know what, there's not one thing listed for the twelfth floor!"

"It sure is secretive, all right. Do you suppose a spy ring could rent that whole floor and pass everything off as normal? Who would know?"

"Maybe Mary Ann found out about it and they had to get rid of her."

"How about that gal up there—she looks just like Hedy Lamarr!"

"At least we found out the bachelor's name: Aaron Seacrest. That was lucky. Quick thinking on your part to give her a fake name, 'Donald'."

"You too, 'Gerald'," said Dave.

For a moment the two were speechless as they continued their walk toward home. Then Dave spoke, "OK, so we got his name. So what? We don't know anything else except he works in a mysterious place. We don't know what he does. If we go back there, we won't learn anything because they won't let anyone beyond that first room. So what the hell do we do now?"

Silence. The two continued walking.

"Let's walk home," said Jake, "I don't feel like waiting for that bus."

The two turned down Lake Avenue and headed toward the bridge and their homes, heads down, thinking but not solving their dilemma. What more could they do?

After several blocks, Dave said, "Let's keep an eye on his house when he comes home every night. Maybe we could even sneak around and peak in when it's dark. We might even see a short-wave radio in there."

Jake nodded in unenthusiastic agreement.

Reaching their split-up point, the two agreed to meet the next day and make further plans, then, disheartened, walked their separate paths home.

Well, we got his name, anyway, thought Dave. Aaron Seacrest. Hmmm. Doesn't sound like a killer.

CHAPTER 8

35 mph speed limit in Minnesota

Duluth News Tribune, Summer, 1943

Watching the bachelor's house ("Aaron's place", as they now called it) was exciting the first evening. At 5:00 P.M. they took their posts in a neighbor's hedge, unseen but still able to peer out and view the entire front of the building. Settling back into his hedge-nest, Dave spied something unusual on Aaron's porch, an irregularly-shaped object the size of a grapefruit, beside the door.

"What is that thing?" he whispered to his partner.

"What thing?" said Jake.

"That big dark thing on the porch. Looks sorta like a football. Ever see anything like that?"

Jake studied for a minute then said, "Can't tell from here. I'll go over and have a close look. Aaron shouldn't be here for a while yet."

"Not now!" said Dave, "Wait 'til tomorrow when we know he won't be home," but it was too late. Jake was on his way.

Dave stared down the street and saw in the distance an approaching vehicle, too big for a car. It's probably the bus bringing Aaron to his home. He'll be here in a minute, discover Jake snooping, drag him into his house, slam the door and Jake will never be seen again! Oh, no… no, it isn't a bus, just a big truck.

Jake returned. "It's an agate, biggest one I've ever seen. Looks like he uses it for a doorstop."

Finding agates on the Point was not unusual; many people had jars full of the colorful, striped pebbles, but they had never seen one that large. Was that agate a sign for something sinister? Perhaps a signal to other spies? Forget it. A bus pulled up, squeaked open its front door, and Aaron stepped out.

The suspect went directly to his house and disappeared inside. The boys kept their distance and settled back for a period of surveillance. When the evening light finally faded, the amateur detectives felt less conspicuous and edged closer to the house, using the surrounding bushes to cover their movements. A few feet from the porch they heard a distant voice, an excited voice, coming from inside. Could it be Berlin calling? Was that a Nip having trouble saying his "l's"? Not moving, not breathing, they strained their ears carefully, and heard—the voice of Gabriel Heatter proclaiming "There's good news tonight, folks!"

Gabriel Heatter! The radio commentator! Aaron was just listening to a standard American radio program. No German or Jap accents. No clickety-click of a code machine. Just Gabriel Heatter.

Dave felt the tension in his body slowly ease and he settled back into his position in the hedge.

"Maybe it's just cover noise so we can't hear his conversation with Berlin," said Jake.

Dave looked at his pal but said nothing. A nearby cricket began chirping and the early adrenaline rush faded away. A single car drove past them; the night settled into silence.

During the next half hour the car traffic faded to zero, the lone cricket became silent, and the radio voices disappeared.

"Let's go," said Dave. "We can come back tomorrow night."

"Maybe we could get inside sometime during the day and search the joint," said Jake.

Dave said nothing but did not like the idea of illegal entry, at least not yet. They could discuss that later. The two arose, agreed to continue their surveillance the next night, and headed their separate ways toward home.

CHAPTER 9

Duluth Is Declared Possible Air Target

Duluth News Tribune, Summer, 1943

The second night of observation from the bushes was a replica of the first. Aaron came home, turned the radio on, turned the radio off, then became totally silent. Two cars drove by. The cricket failed to chirp.

Night three was a duplicate of two and night four yielded more of the same. Jake said it was as dull as Mrs. Grady's love life, a reference to their unmarried history teacher who wore long grey dresses, kept her hair in a tight bun, and balanced a small pair of glasses on her outsized nose. Dave agreed that nothing productive happened yet, but they should give it a few more days.

"OK," said Jake, "but next Tuesday we pry open a window and give the place a once-over." Dave reluctantly agreed.

On the fifth night the boys settled into their hedge hideout and impatiently waited for Aaron's bus. The vehicle arrived, the doors creaked open, Aaron stepped down, and instead of striding straight to his home, turned back with outstretched hand and assisted a young lady from the bus.

"It's 'Hedy Lamarr' !" said Jake.

The girl from Aaron's workplace stepped off and walked hand-in-hand with their quarry to the little house. Aaron extracted a key from his pocket, unlocked the door, and the smiling couple disappeared inside.

"My god," said Jake, "do you suppose she's in on the plot too?!"

"Hold on, Jake, she could be as innocent as Mary Ann; she might end up dead tonight!"

The two paused to think over what was happening. Maybe "Hedy" was a fellow conspirator, but if she wasn't, someone ought to protect her, at least warn her.

"Think we should call the police?" said Jake.

"What do we tell them? That Aaron just disappeared into his house with a young lady and we are sure he's going to kill her? We don't know any of that, Jake. For all we know they are both innocent."

"Ha!" replied Jake, "that guy is the killer and you know it! The only question is if she helped."

"So what do we do?"

In the next minute it all became clear what they had to do. The backside door of the house opened and the young couple stepped out and marched back to Aaron's little sailboat tethered in the bay. They clambered aboard, shoved off, and began to unfurl the sails for a trip—somewhere.

"We've got to follow them, DA."

"Our little boat would never keep up."

"But we could see where they go if they don't head out into the lake. It's worth a try. Maybe Aaron will try to drown her out behind the island."

Dave glanced at the little island just off the shore of Park Point. It consisted of mostly sand, was fringed with brush along the shoreline, and housed nothing but seabirds. It obstructed their view, for sure.

"OK., but we can't go out too far. 'The Titanic' is good in calm water, but she could never take the big waves." Nodding agreement, they leaped from the hedge and raced back to the hidden boat.

A block from Aaron's house sat an empty lot containing tall weeds, grass, and the rotting remains of a burned house. It was there, some six months earlier, that Jake discovered in the weeds a discarded mortar box, six feet long and covered with crusty concrete.

Jake quickly informed Dave and the two of them immediately saw the possibilities for a boat. The sides were only ten inches high and she did leak a little after the layers of concrete were removed, but she did float and supported Jake and Dave. The boys nicknamed her "The Titanic" and whittled paddles from old boards to propel the little skiff. Many trips were taken from the Point to the deserted little island just a hundred yards off-shore in the bay.

On reaching the vacant lot, the boys dragged "The Titanic" out of the tall weeds that kept her hidden, grabbed their paddles that had been concealed beneath their craft, and launched the boat next to aging pilings that had at one time supported a boat house.

Dave sat in the front and Jake, the heavier of the two, clambered in behind him. The first few strokes of their paddles moved them several feet off shore.

"There she is!" said Dave.

The sail of Aaron's craft puffed out, filled with the slight breeze of late afternoon, and the sloop headed toward the south end of the island.

"Let's row," said Jake, and the two young sailors/detectives propelled their craft southward in pursuit of their quarry.

"She's headed around the island, for sure," said Jake, "Good thing we got out here."

The two paddled hard but the little sailboat gradually pulled away from them, circled the south end of the island, and began to curl back north, around the island and out of the boys' sight.

"C'mon, DA, push that paddle!"

Reaching the south end of the island, the boys regained sight of the sloop as it bent around the far side. Both passengers were still in the sailboat. Then it was out of sight again.

"DA, we've got to go further out in the bay. He may dump her anytime now and no one will ever know it."

"OK, Jake, but you're the one who can't swim, and we've never taken this baby out in those waves."

"This old tub will hold up just fine, DA, and we've got to protect Hedy from that kraut spy."

Around the south end of the island the waves grew in size. Paddling into the rough water of the bay, Dave noticed the bigger waves breaking over the low sides of their craft. Water began to accumulate on the floor.

"Jake, we've got to turn around, we're filling with water!"

In the following seconds, before the boys could react, two major events occurred: They suddenly saw their sailboat quarry coming back and bearing straight toward them. At the same time, a large wave elevated their small craft, tipped it on its side, and deposited the two passengers into the icy waters.

Dave went head-first into the bay and momentarily felt paralyzed by the extreme cold of the lake that never warms. Surfacing after several seconds, he gasped for breath and looked for Jake. Neither his partner nor the Titanic was visible. He called out. No answer. He began to swim in circles, peering underwater. The cold water began to stiffen his arms and legs and his paddling slowed. Where is Jake? Where is Jake? His limbs became immovable; his mind began to fog. The ultimate drive for survival seeped from his body and he stopped fighting. The bitter cold ebbed, replaced by a welcome warmth. He relaxed, his mind no longer fearful. Slowly, slowly reality slipped away, not to darkness but to a light, soft, wondrous world of rest.

CHAPTER 10

3 Jap Attacks on West Coast Are Bared

Duluth News Tribune, Summer, 1943

"This one is coming around," said a distant voice. Dave opened his eyes and found himself looking directly into the face of… Aaron Seacrest. Aaron Seacrest, "the Bachelor," the accused murderer and German spy, the man who now hovered over him in soaking clothes, wet hair pushed back over his head

Dave struggled to rise but his body was not yet maneuverable. "Where's Jake?" he asked.

"Is that your buddy? He's up on the bow. Got a nasty gash on his arm. Must have banged it on the boat when you two got dumped. He hasn't revived yet."

Directly above Dave a sail fluttered in the breeze. I'm in Aaron's sloop, he thought. Glancing toward the bow, Dave could see Hedy kneeling over the unmoving form of someone, someone protected by a coat that Aaron had been wearing.

Dave attempted to get up again, reached one knee, slipped, and fell back to the deck. He shivered violently, curled like a fetus, and passed out.

CHAPTER 11

Penicillin Scarce

Duluth News Tribune, Summer, 1943

Dave awakened to find his worried mother Tena talking quietly with a nurse. He glanced around the white room wondering what time it was and how long he had been there. Turning to his mother he greeted her in the strongest voice he could muster, "Good morning, Ma."

Mrs. Aune turned quickly to her son's bed. "Davey, thank God you're all right! Do you feel OK? Are you warm enough? What were you boys doing way out there anyway? Thank God that Mr. Seacrest was there to fish you two out."

She grabbed his hands and hung on tightly.

The events of the previous night came slowly back to him. He remembered the plunge into the water, the search for Jake, the image of his pal lying unconscious in the little sloop. "Where's Jake?" he asked.

"He's just down the hall, dear, in another room. I think his mother is with him. How do you feel?"

Good question. He didn't hurt anywhere. Stirring his body slightly, he checked for damage. Everything seemed fine. "I'm good, Ma, let's get out of here."

"The doctor will be here shortly and, if he thinks you're OK, we can go."

Dave thought of Jake and remembered Aaron's remark about a gash on the arm. "Is Jake awake yet, Ma?"

"I don't know, son. Maybe we can stop and see him when we go."

Then she started with the questions again, slower this time, with pauses begging for answers. Dave answered some, skirted others, and shrugged off a few with an "I don't know."

Fifteen minutes later, much to Dave's relief, the doctor entered and put an end to his mother's interrogation. "How are you this morning, young fella? Had quite an adventure, eh? Can you sit up on the edge of your bed?" Dave sat obediently while the man moved his cold stethoscope over Dave's torso, pausing now and then to giving breathing instructions.

The doctor turned to Mrs. Aune. "He seems to be just fine. The sleep he got last night was just what he needed. Take him home, keep an eye on him, but I think he'll be back to normal by this afternoon. If there are any complications, let me know."

"How's Jake?" Dave asked.

"Is that your friend? He's doing pretty good now. I talked to him a few minutes ago. He's a little groggy yet and he has that gash on his arm so we're going to keep him here for awhile, but he should be OK. Stop in and see him on your way out—it would be good for him."

A feeling of relief swept over Dave. Yeah, let's get out of this room and stop to see Jake. "When can I leave?"

"It will take a few minutes for the paperwork, but you can get dressed now and the nurse will be back to dismiss you."

Dave dressed hurriedly then sat impatiently waiting for his release. The nurse finally arrived, Mrs. Aune went to the main desk to take care of the paperwork, and Dave got the location of his pal and sped off in search.

Turning quickly into Jake's room, Dave spotted his pal, eyes open but looking flushed and uncomfortable. Jake's mother sat rigidly in a nearby chair, hands folded in her lap and concern etching her face. Dressed in a simple, faded housedress, she looked like a poster child for the depression. Strange, Dave thought, this is one of the few times I've seen her without looking through a screen door. Jake never invited him inside their house. She studied Dave, nodded her head in greeting, but said nothing.

"Hey, how you doin'?" Dave spoke to his wounded comrade.

"I'm good," said Jake, "where's our boat?"

"I don't know; guess I'll have to go looking for it," Dave replied, but as he spoke his friend's eyes closed and his breathing became audible. A feeling of dread spread through Dave's body.

A nurse appeared from nowhere, stepped into the room, and said he would have to leave. Dave asked her how his pal was doing and she eyed him condescendingly and said, "He's not feeling good right now. He needs rest."

She stared at him coldly waiting for him to leave.

Perhaps the young lady wanted to protect the privacy of her patient. Maybe she didn't know the answers but wouldn't admit it. Possibly she didn't think talking to a young boy was worth the effort. Dave paused for a moment not knowing what to do or say. Finally, he waved good-by to Mrs. Anderson and stepped into the hall where he met his approaching mother. The two of them walked silently out of the hospital, Dave staring at the floor, tired, fearful, and frustrated knowing only that his best friend was "not feeling good" and that "he needs rest." On reaching home, Dave discovered he also "needed rest."

The following morning, Dave arose and noted some stiffness in his legs. Probably due to that cold water, he thought. His mother greeted him, "How are you today, Davey?"

"Fine, Ma. I want to grab some breakfast and go see Jake."

"I understand, but don't overdo it. You don't have any aches or pains?"

"No, Ma, I'm just fine, but I have to check on Jake." Dave grabbed some bread and milk, wolfed them down, and headed out the door. "See you for lunch."

Mrs. Aune shook her head but said nothing and returned to her floor sweeping.

Dave hopped the first bus that came along, not wanting to waste time by walking. Jumping off downtown, he moved quickly, sometimes running, to the hospital. Ignoring the hospital personnel, he headed directly for the stairs leading to the second floor and Jake's room.

"Hold it there, Sunshine!" a voice called out. Dave turned and saw an older woman standing behind the main desk and staring directly at him. "Visiting hours don't start until ten o'clock, so you just better sit for awhile. The lounge is over there," she said, pointing to her right.

"Sorry," Dave said, and moved toward the designated area, a room whose perimeter was filled with small tables, numerous lamps, and soft easy chairs. He sat down, looked for a magazine, and heard a strange voice from a dark corner:

"Hi, Dave. You may not recognize me, but my name is Aaron Seacrest."

CHAPTER 12

Tennis Courts Turned Into Chicken Farms

Duluth News Tribune, Summer, 1943

"How you doing? I must say you look a lot better today than the last time I saw you."

"Good morning," Dave stammered, "I just came in to see my buddy Jake."

"Me too," said Aaron, "I stopped by yesterday and found out you had gone home but your pal was still here. That gash on his arm is apparently infected and giving him some trouble. But you probably know all that."

My god, thought Dave, the killer knows more about my buddy's health than I do. "Yeah, I guess so, but he's going to be OK."

"Do you remember me, Dave? I'm the guy who fished you out of the water."

"Yessir, I remember. Thank you." Why is this murderer here?

"We can get in to see your pal in a couple minutes. I can't stay too long—have to get back to work. You know where I work, right? Margaret said you two had stopped in one day to say hello to me."

"Margaret?"

"Yeah, Margaret Lorese. She works in our office and was sailing with me when we saw you go for a swim."

"Oh, yeah, we did stop in one day. Jake and I have seen you on the Point several times, saw you disappear into that big building, and decided to just follow and say hello." Dave paused, wet his dry lips, and waited. Would Aaron believe that story?

At that moment a nurse stepped into the lounge, announcing to the waiting visitors, "You folks can go in now."

Saved by the bell.

Dave followed Aaron through the hallway and up the stairs. He looks like a good person, Dave thought. Of course, you can't go on appearances. Hitler's not bad looking either if he'd shave off that silly little mustache.

Reaching Jake's room, Dave stepped inside and felt a coolness he had not noted the day before. The shade over the single window was pulled down, the weak light in the room came from a small corner lamp, and the silence was broken only by the sounds of their footsteps. Mrs. Andersen sat rigidly in the same chair where she had been the day before, wearing the same dress and the same expression. Did she ever go home?

Turning toward the bed, Dave stared at his old pal whose eyes were closed and who was breathing noisily.

"Is he sleeping, Mrs. Anderson?" She nodded.

Aaron said nothing but gazed at Jake with a troubled expression. Turning to Dave he said, "Maybe we should go. It looks like your buddy needs some rest."

Dave didn't answer, but the two of them said good-bye to Mrs. Anderson who again nodded silently and stared at her son. They walked from the room and down the hall. It wasn't until they reached the lobby that Dave asked Aaron what he thought of Jake's condition.

"I think he'll be just fine, Dave." Aaron smiled as he spoke, but Dave heard an uncertainty in his voice and noted that his eyebrows were pulled down over his eyes. It was the same face he had seen when his dad told him that his dog Skipper had been hit by a car but would be "just fine." Skipper died a day later.

Aaron pushed open the main entrance door and continued, "I know he looks kind of tough right now, but he's young and strong and the rest will do him a world of good. God knows we don't need another tragedy on the Point. Did you know the girl that was killed?" Dave nodded but did not speak.

"I got back from Washington a couple days after it happened and couldn't believe it. A murder right here in Duluth. We've got enough troubles in this world without that."

Dave's pace faltered and his head snapped to the side to stare at his escort. *He was in Washington?* Aaron gazed back, studied his young cohort intently, then stopped walking. For several seconds he peered fixedly at the boy. Finally he spoke.

"Did you think I had something to do with that murder, Dave?"

CHAPTER 13

4 Ships Launched At Zenith Ship Yards

Duluth News Tribune, Summer, 1943

Dave was speechless. He stared, mouth agape, but the words wouldn't come. Finally, he mumbled, "No, not really, we were, you know, kinda looking at everybody involved... she was a good friend and, well, we wanted to, ah, see if we could, you know, sorta..."

Aaron interrupted. "I understand, Dave. Look, if I was in your situation I certainly would have been suspicious. Listen, how about you come down to my office right now and talk to my supervisor. He can verify my story. It would give you some peace of mind about me and I would feel a lot better if I wasn't one of your suspects. I'd like to be your friend."

Dave again was short on words. After a short pause, he nodded and said, "Sure, that's fine. You don't have to do that, but, O.K., if it will make you feel better."

Aaron smiled, turned, and headed downtown with his young friend in tow.

The next half-hour blurred together as Dave's mind attempted to grasp what was happening. They walked to the office building, rode the elevator, and heard the cheery greeting of Margaret Lorese. Then an introduction to Mr. Schneider (Sideholm? Sidler?), Aaron's boss. Aaron related the story of Mary Ann's death and Mr. S gladly corroborated Aaron's story. "Oh, yes, terrible thing that death! Read about it in the paper. Yes, Aaron was off to Washington during that time. My goodness, I do hope they get the killer!" More small talk and then it ended. Some pleasant farewells and Dave walked back into the elevator.

A few minutes later he found himself walking down Superior Street, staring at the cracks in the sidewalk, and wondering what to do next. His good friend lay in a coma, solving Mary Ann's murder seemed more unlikely than ever, the War still blazed overseas, and a cool wind blew off the lake on a bleak day. Not a moment of buoyant optimism. What now? he thought, and began a slow hike home.

CHAPTER 14

Zoot Suits Riot In Los Angeles

Duluth News Tribune, Summer, 1943

Dave lay in his bed, half asleep, even though the morning was drawing to a close. What reason did he have to get up? It's a miserable world, he thought. They can all go to hell. Then a cry shattered the silence: "Davey, Davey, look at this!"

His mother's shout, a sound he seldom heard from the normally undemonstrative woman, got his attention. He popped out of bed and walked to the kitchen. "What is it, Ma?"

"It's in today's paper, dear. They just arrested some young sailor in connection with Mary Ann's death!"

Dave was stunned. He took the paper from his mother and quickly scanned the news article. A young sailor who had been on leave at the time of the murder, had been in trouble with the law in his teen-age years, and who had been seen drinking heavily on the fateful night was in jail. He read the page again, looking for the few facts disclosed. "They don't say much, Ma."

"They never do, dear. The police have to keep some things secret for the trial."

Dave studied the article again. God, I hope they got the right guy, he thought, and went back to his bedroom to get dressed.

Following a brief breakfast, Dave left the house looking to talk to someone other than his mother. It was at moments like this that he missed his pal Jake; they could talk about anything. They understood one another. Even when they disagreed they were still good friends. Right now, Dave would even talk to Birdy if he happened to show up. He continued his slow saunter, staring at the cracks in the sidewalk, his mind confused in a myriad of thoughts

"Davey! Davey! Come on up here. I need your help!"

Dave's sluggish walk down the sidewalk had taken him in front of Scotty's house, and the old man stood on his porch apparently working on some project and waving to his young friend. Maybe he's not mad about the car incident, Dave thought, and headed up to check on the old man.

As Dave approached the porch, he saw three mirrors (from cars?), a handful of screws, a screwdriver, and a hammer scattered about the tiny deck. What in the world? he thought, but didn't have to wait long for an explanation.

"Lookee here, Davey, yesterday morning I missed my bus again. You remember it was misting a little so I sat here on the porch waiting for that blasted vehicle to arrive and she went right on by! I waved, but it didn't help, fer crissake! They want me to go right down to the curb and stand in the rain and wait. I'll catch pneumonia! I could see the bus coming if it wasn't for those trees Mrs. Bulinsky has in her yard."

Dave could see the problem. The house sat back from the street about fifty feet and visibility was obscured by the trees next door. The bus wasn't visible until it was practically in front of Scotty's house. Scotty continued.

"I've had these old mirrors in my cellar for some time and figure it's time to put them to use. I want to arrange them on the porch railing so they'll reflect the image of the bus when it's way up the street. That'll give me time to get to the curb and flag that baby down."

"You want to put a mirror on the railing so it will show you when the bus is coming?"

"Right! Now I got these other mirrors to help if necessary, to bend the light just the right way, but I haven't figured out the proper angles yet."

Dave surveyed the situation. The railing sat about two feet in front of Scotty's chair. Dave put his head directly above the railing and peered to his left in the direction of any approaching bus. Trees. All he saw was trees. Moving forward two feet did nothing to increase the visibility. Dave scratched his head and pondered the situation.

"Mr. O'Doul, I can't figure out how that mirror is going to help any. It doesn't look like the mirror could see any better than you from your chair."

"Ah, Davey, you see, that's the beauty of mirrors. They bend the light in all directions. I got three old car mirrors here and if we can just put 'em in the right places, we'll be able to see way down the street. I need you to hold one of those babies, or maybe both of them, while I move the biggest one around to get the right angle. After we figure out the right spots, I'll screw them into place and we'll have the problem solved."

"Are you sure this will work, Mr. O'Doul?"

"Well, of course I am, Davey! I haven't lived all these years for nothin'. And remember I'm half English, half Irish, and full of scotch! Ha, ha, ha!"

The sight of the little, old man with his balding head shining in the light and his belly shaking with laughter was too much. Mr. O'Doul's loud guffaw and the twinkle in his eye told Dave that any further argument was useless.

"Where do you want me to hold these two?"

"Let's start out right there on the middle of the railing with one; let's not use the other one unless we have to."

Dave grabbed a mirror and held it just above the railing. Scotty took the biggest of the three and began moving it about, peering, shaking his head, and mumbling to himself.

"That's not quite right," he said, and continued viewing the mirror from different angles. "Hold yours a little higher."

Dave obeyed, hoisting his mirror two feet above the railing. Scotty continued his quest, moving up and down, left and right. "Looks like we'll have to use that third one too," he said, grabbing the second mirror in his left hand and maneuvering the two of them through various positions.

Dave continued to follow orders, moving his mirror through every position Scotty asked for. No luck. Finally Scotty lost his patience. "Ah, fer crissake, there's got to be something wrong with these mirrors, Davey! I've got a couple other bigger ones in the cellar and maybe tomorrow we can try this again. OK?"

Dave nodded his acceptance, thankful the session was at least temporarily over, and backed down the steps to the lawn. "See you later, Mr. O'Doul!"

Dave walked away smiling, his blues having vanished in a flurry of useless maneuvering. Those mirrors didn't reflect the buses but they did brighten his attitude.

That night, before going to sleep, Dave took note of his situation. His buddy was in the hospital, still unconscious, but still breathing and Dave knew he would recover. A sailor was arrested for the murder of Mary Ann so maybe that mystery would be solved and the murderer brought to justice. Dave pondered his options. OK, so what can I do now? Maybe it's time for that nocturnal excursion Jake and I planned a few months ago.

CHAPTER 15

Our Boys Need 2 Tons Of Scrap From Every Farm

Duluth News Tribune, Summer, 1943

Mr. Brastad ("The Bastard") owned a metal statue of a toad that sat in the center of his lawn. It stood at least three feet tall and glared out menacingly at all passersby who walked down the sidewalk in front of the house. Jake and Dave decided that since everyone was making sacrifices for the war, The Bastard should too: That toad should be donated to a metal drive. "You could probably build two tanks from that beast," said Jake, and Dave agreed. It wouldn't be easy to get the amphibian; it would require a covert, late-night outing, but it would be well worth it. Dave would now do it on his own as a tribute to his pal; Jake would approve and it would probably help his recovery.

Dave lay awake that night watching the minutes slip by. Lying in bed he went over his plans carefully; he pictured himself a Marine, planning a raid: Wait until midnight, silently leave the house, and walk to Bastard's house. Under cover of darkness, crawl to the middle of the yard, grab the toad, and stealthily creep back to the sidewalk. Carry toadie two blocks away so Bastard won't immediately discover him, and place him on the curb under the other junk that would be picked up in the metal drive the next morning. Perfect.

Midnight finally arrived. Slipping out of the house was no problem since Dave's folks always retired early and their bedroom was at the back of the house.

Wearing his darkest clothes, Dave walked as quietly as possible toward his objective.

Darkness infested the scene. A cloudy sky covered any stars that had hopes of brightening the night, and most houses had no illumination. Those few homes that did maintain a light had their blackout curtains drawn so that few lumens escaped. Street lights were turned off early every evening. Thus, the main source of light came from low-hanging clouds that reflected the leftover blush from downtown where several businesses kept their signature signs aglow. Dave carefully picked his way through the inkiness and neared his objective.

He could barely make out the outline of the Brastad house as he paused by the hedge on the edge of the lawn. The house gave no indication of life, no sound, no light. Dropping to his knees, he crawled under the bushes to the grass beyond and , as he emerged, wondered if any creature could hear his pounding heart. Slowly he slithered forward, straining his eyes and ears for any activity. Now he could see the rough outline of toadie and his heart hammered even more. A few more feet and I'll grab the ugly beast, thought Dave. Squirming forward, he turned on his left side and prepared to grab the gargoyle. Then the yard light came on.

Wartime is a great teacher. From watching newsreels and army movies you learn to stride forward when thrusting a bayonet, to start a grenade throw from behind your ear, and to squeeze the trigger, not jerk it. And, you learn to freeze in position and close one eye if a flare is unexpectedly fired at night. When the porch light came on, Dave stopped moving and closed his left eye.

Fortunately for the invader, his body lay almost entirely in the shadow of toadie. He lay quiet, holding his breath, as the screen door on the big house squeaked open. From his position, Dave could not see what was happening, but the options raced through his mind: get up and run, *now*; wait until The Bastard came into the yard and perhaps looked another direction and then run; or, stay perfectly still and trust in the darkness. He opted for the last choice.

The door made a noise when it was opened but no slamming or further racket ensued. Did he close the door silently? Was he now approaching the prostrate figure? Seconds ticked by. Surely he can hear my heart beat!

Finally a brief squeak followed by a bang as the door closed. Did that mean he went back in or was he now advancing into the yard? Dave didn't move but strained to hear any other noises. Silence. Then the light went out.

Dave maintained his position for a period of time—10 seconds? 30 seconds? a minute? It felt like an hour as his body began to cramp and the cold crept into his bones. Finally, he could take it no longer, rolled onto his stomach, and carefully, fearfully, lifted his head until the house came into view. No people in sight, no motion anywhere. Dave relaxed onto the ground, pulled his watch from his pocket, checked the time, decided to wait thirty minutes before moving, and let his body relax onto the moist grass.

Time stood still. Dave waited for what he thought was ten minutes, checked his watch, and determined that less than three minutes had expired. His mind wandered: Mary Ann was such a fine girl. Damn, I hope they caught the right guy! What about Jake? How long before he regains consciousness? Maybe he won't. Naw, I can't think that way. Wait 'til I tell him about this outing. He's going to be really pleased. Why did I come here by myself? I should have waited for Jake. Tick, tick, tick. The seconds dragged by as the cold from the dew-laden ground seeped into his body. Five minutes left. Three. One.

Dave's chilled body rebelled as he eased up to peak over toadie. All looked quiet. Slowly he reached out to grab the top of the statue and pull it toward him. This is a heavy beast, he thought; I hope I can carry it. Getting to his knees and wrapping both hands around toadie, he gave a push, struggled to his feet and discovered he could lift the ugly, metal figure. Lugging the heavy load, he staggered back to the hedge, put toadie down, crawled under the bushes, and then dragged the creature under the barrier. So far, so good.

Dave regained his feet and hoisted the statue to one hip. Then he unsteadily wobbled down the sidewalk. One block to go, but I have time and should make that without any trouble, he thought. Then he spotted a man in the distance slowly limping toward him.

Thinking quickly, Dave stepped back onto a set of five steps that descended from the lawn of a darkened house. The steps sat between the ends of hedges that surrounded the lawn. Placing toadie on the third step, he removed his jacket and wrapped it around the statue. Next he placed his cap on the head of the amphibian and pulled it down so little could be seen of the face. Then he sat down next to the robed gargoyle and waited.

As the man approached, Dave recognized the gait as that of Mr. Black, an old carpenter with a bad leg. As far as Dave knew, he was a good man, worked in his garage making cabinets, lived quietly with his wife, and sometimes took nocturnal strolls because of the pain in his bad leg. Wonder how he got the crippled leg?, Dave thought, but now a better question was, How good is his eyesight?

Mr. Black slowly hobbled closer, his limp more noticeable than Dave had ever noticed before. Extra pain at night? He stopped in front of Dave. "What are you boys doing out at this hour?"

"Hi, Mr. Black," hoping that familiarity would reduce suspicion; he knew Mr. Black but was sure Mr. Black didn't know him. "Me and my brother are staying out in our tent tonight and my little brother couldn't sleep so we decided to take a little walk." He placed his right arm around his "little brother" and smiled.

Mr. Black studied the pair sitting in the darkness, his countenance remaining severe, his head moving, trying to get a better look at the boys on the steps. "Well, you two better go back to your tent. It's not safe out here for you. Remember what happened to that young girl a little while back."

"Yessir," said Dave. "We're just going to sit here and rest for a minute then head straight back."

Mr. Black continued his surveillance of the pair, started to speak, stopped, harrumphed, then turned and continued his painful hike. Dave sat quietly as his heartbeat slowed to near normal.

As soon as Mr. Black disappeared from sight, Dave retrieved his cap and jacket from toadie, placed the ugly burden on his hip, and continued his own hobbling down the sidewalk.

The rest was easy. He reached the pile of recyclable metal, lay toadie on its back next to the pile, and covered the amphibian with a few squashed cans and a ragged piece of sheet metal taken from the junk pile. Done.

Thirty minutes later, Dave lay in his bed recalling his adventure. Too bad Jake wasn't along, he thought. I'll tell him all about it tomorrow. And he slept.

CHAPTER 16

Blackous No More Than Monthly

Duluth News Tribune, Summer, 1943

Morning broke with bright sunshine and renewed hope. Toadie was taken care of, Mary Ann's murderer sat in custody, and Dave felt sure that Jake would soon revive. Perhaps if Jake heard the successful toadie story it would speed his recovery.

"Davey, breakfast is ready!"

The sound of his mother's voice made Dave stop and think about her: she had a worried look in her eyes as her son coped with his depression. He had noticed the concern but did nothing about it. He was too concerned with himself. Well, time to change that.

"Morning, Ma!" Dave's loud greeting and cheerful demeanor shocked his mother, and she stared at her grinning son. "What a beautiful morning! I'm going downtown and see Jake, maybe tell him some stories. One of these days he's going to sit right up and smile. I know it. Maybe today!"

Mrs. Aune stared in disbelief. Was this the same boy who was moping around yesterday? She smiled at her son and sat down. "I think you're right, Davey. One of these days Jake will be just fine, but remember it may be a while yet." She picked up her cup of coffee, had a long sip, and Dave thought he could see some tension leaving her body.

"Guess I'll have a piece of toast," he said. He grabbed a slice of bread, pulled down the door of the toaster, inserted the bread, closed the toaster, and plugged in the cord. A minute later he partially opened the door on the toaster, watched as the bread slid down and reversed sides, then deftly re-closed the door. "Someday they'll make a toaster that does both sides of the bread at once," he said. After another minute, Dave opened the toaster and removed his toast which displayed a golden brown on both sides. "Pretty good, hey, Ma!"

Mrs. Aune smiled as she watched her son spread white margarine on the toast. "When this war is over, you can have real butter, Davey. And maybe things will settle down some." She was clearly relieved.

Dave wolfed down his toast and told his mother he was leaving. "I'm headed up to the hospital, Ma. Not sure when I'll get back." Then he walked to his mother, gave her a kiss on the cheek, turned, and walked out the door. Tena was stunned. Her son hadn't kissed her good-bye for many years.

Dave bounded up the stairs at the hospital with renewed energy. Perhaps the news of toadie's abduction would awaken his old pal. Turning from the hallway into Jake's room, Dave noted Mrs. Anderson sitting in her usual spot by the window, wearing her usual dress, and greeting him with her usual, non-reactive stare. "Good morning, Mrs. Anderson," he said, and caught sight of a dark figure sitting on the opposite side of the room. It was Buck Anderson, Jake's dad!

Taken aback, Dave hesitated for a moment, then greeted the seldom seen parent, "Hello, Mr. Anderson. Nice to see you." Buck nodded his head slightly, but made no other response. What's he doing here? Dave thought, and then reconsidered. He's here to see his son, of course! Why now? Why wasn't he here before? He looks thinner than the last time I saw him, although his clothes are cleaner. He probably got dressed up for this hospital visit.

Getting no conversation from either parent, Dave turned to Jake who appeared to be simply sleeping in his bed. "Jake," Dave said, "remember that plan we had for Mr. Brastad?" (He carefully used the real name in front of the Anderson parents.) "Well, mission accomplished!" He knew that he could get in trouble if Buck or Martha questioned him about the "mission," but he doubted that either of them would speak. He pondered what else to say. I want to get Jake to wake up, he thought, but I can't confess to a crime in front of the Anderson parents who probably wouldn't understand. Then, as he stood wondering what to do, his dilemma was solved. Jake opened his eyes and said, "So you got toadie. Nice work."

"Jake!" Mrs. Anderson shouted as she leaped from her chair, flew across the room, and buried her head in her son's shoulder. "Jake, Jake," she called as her body shook with sobs of relief. "My boy, my boy! Thank God!"

Buck Anderson stood up with a look of amazement and slowly moved toward his son. He reached the bed, grabbed his son's hand and said, "Jake, I'm so sorry. Thank God you're awake! I'll be a better dad, I promise. We have a lot to make up for."

Dave took a step backward as the two parents rushed to their son. He wanted to stay and talk. He wanted to tell Jake how happy he was to see his pal awake again. He wanted to tell him about his toadie adventure. He looked at the trembling body of Mrs. Anderson as she clung to Jake's hand and sobbed uncontrollably. Buck Anderson stood quietly, holding his son's other hand, and tears began to run down his sunken cheeks.

Dave took another step back and spoke quietly. "I have to go now, Jake. I'll see you tomorrow. So long! Goodbye, Andersons."

The Anderson parents either didn't hear him or were too absorbed to pay any attention. Dave turned and walked quietly from the hospital room, down the hall and the steps, and out the main entrance to the building. He paused outside, leaned his suddenly-weary body against the cold grey stone of the structure, dropped his head to his chest, and sobbed silently by himself. It had been a long struggle.

A few moments later, the young man straightened his shoulders, wiped his eyes with back of his hand, cleared his throat, took a deep breath, and began a long, slow walk back home. The worst was over; or so he thought.

CHAPTER 17

When Dave arose the next morning, he found the temperature already above seventy and a hazy sky the color of an old penny. He gazed out the window of his room at the strange weather and noted that fog was beginning to roll in off the big lake. Heavy fog.

Walking into the kitchen, Dave greeted his mother and noted that she was watching him closely. He would have to be upbeat. No sense in worrying her anymore.

"Funny looking weather out there, Ma. What's happening?"

"I don't know, Davey, but it does look a little weird. Turn the radio on and see if we can get a weather report."

Dave strode to the old *Motorola,* turned the *On* switch, and waited impatiently as the machine warmed to its task. Within a few seconds the mellow voices of the *Andrews Sisters* filled the room and Dave had to turn the volume down.

"Nice song," said Mrs. Aune.

"Yeah, nice song," said Dave.

"Davey, maybe it would be better if you didn't go visit Jake today. You know, give the family a chance to settle down and get re-acquainted. Then maybe tomorrow you could go visit. And you'd probably have more time to talk to him, too."

Dave thought about that. He had told his mother what happened yesterday, how he didn't get a chance to talk with Jake. He hoped to go see his pal today. "I suppose you're right, Ma; you usually are."

Mrs. Aune smiled at her son. The boy was growing up.

The *Andrews Sisters* finished their song and the *KDAL* announcer spoke up, "Folks, we have a news bulletin here, just in. It says that the police have just arrested a new suspect in the Park Point, Mary Ann Pleason murder case. The identity of the new suspect has not yet been released. Please stay tuned to this station for further developments." And with that, *Bing Crosby* began to croon about his long, lost love.

Mrs. Aune stared apprehensively at her son and said, "Well, they're still working hard on the case, Davey."

Dave stared out the living room window. "I hope they've got the right guy this time." He paused a few seconds. "We didn't get that weather report yet. Come on, guys," he said to the radio, "tell us about this weird weather!"

And, as if on command, the announcer spoke, "You folks have probably noticed the strange looking sky over the Twin Ports, today. The old weatherman tells us that we have warm air sitting over our cities this morning, but there is a cold front moving in from Canada. If that front moves in quickly, we could get a real good thunderstorm. If it comes in slowly, as it appears to be doing, we will end up with some of the thickest fog we have seen for a long time."

Dave looked at his mother. "Think I'll go work in my room on my model plane."

Mrs. Aune nodded, turned the radio off, and returned to her kitchen.

Just before twelve, she called her son out to a lunch of fried eggs and toast, a meal that filled the air with a pleasant, mouth-watering aroma. Dave hastened out to the kitchen and on the way snapped the *Motorola* back on. "Maybe they'll have some more news on the weather, Ma. That fog is getting as thick as vanilla pudding."

The two sat down to their repast and the *News at Noon* came on: "In our headlines, local man arrested in murder case and the fog is closing down the Twin Ports. Details after these messages."

"Wonder who the local man is, Davey. I hope they give us his name."

"We probably won't know him anyway, Ma."

The ads ended and the announcer came back with his best dramatic voice, "Duluth police today released an earlier suspect and then arrested a local man in connection with the brutal slaying of Mary Ann Pleason of Park Point. The local man, also a Park Point resident, is identified as Brian 'Buck' Anderson."

Dave stopped in mid-chew and stared at his mother. Buck Anderson? Jake's father? They must be talking about another Buck Anderson. It couldn't be the Buck Anderson he knew. There must be some mistake.

But there was no mistake. The report listed Buck's address on the Point and Dave knew it all too well. How could this be? Dave jumped to his feet and began pacing about the kitchen.

"There must be some mistake, Ma, Buck would never do such a thing. He's tough, sure, and he swats Jake once in a while, but he'd never kill anybody!" He continued to walk back and forth in the tiny room.

"You're probably right, Davey. They'll probably turn him loose tomorrow when they get all the facts. He's not the first one they brought in for questioning." She watched fearfully as her son continued his pacing.

"Ma, I've got to go see Jake now. Maybe I can help."

"I understand how you feel, Davey, but you probably shouldn't bother him right now. The family has to figure this out. Besides, he may be out of the hospital now and may be at the jail. Just think how you would act if your dad was in big trouble. They need some time alone."

Dave heard his mother but didn't stop his pacing. Jake needs me now, he thought. I should go see him! But maybe I should leave him alone for awhile. Maybe tomorrow would be better. This must be a mistake. What can I do?

"I'm going back in my room, Ma. Tell me if there's any more news."

Dave went back in his room and closed the door. He sat on the bed. Then he got up and looked at his model plane. Back to the bed. Stare out the window. Pace the floor. What to do. Look at the clock. Sit on the bed.

Then a knock on the door. "Davey, I have a favor to ask you."

Dave opened the door to see his distressed mother, wringing her hands and attempting a smile. "Davey," she said, "I was wondering if I could get you to go downtown on an errand for me. I know it's awfully foggy out there, but I'll give you a couple tokens and you can take the bus back and forth."

Dave hesitated for just a few seconds. "Sure, Ma, I can do that. What do you need?"

Mrs. Aune spoke hurriedly, running her words together, reciting her rehearsed request in a long, breathless statemen: "Well, you know your father's birthday is coming up in a couple weeks and I've been trying to get him a special present and he wants a shovel so he can work over that extra ground and make the garden bigger, but you just can't find any shovels these days—guess they melted them all down for tanks or helmets or something—anyway *Brastad's Hardware* takes in used stuff and re-sells it and Mrs. Torgerson told me they just got some used garden tools and would you go see if you can get a shovel from Mr. Brastad before they're all gone? I'll give you some money." She paused.

Go see The Bastard, Dave thought. Jake's in trouble and I have to go see that miserable old goat. What next? He gazed at the pleading look in his mother's eyes. She's worried about me, he thought, and wants to give me something to do.

"Sure, Ma, I'd be glad to."

Mrs. Aune sighed in relief.

CHAPTER 18

Allies Invade Sicily

Duluth News Tribune, Summer, 1943

Dave stood at the bus stop, shivering in the oppressive fog that hung like a soggy blanket over his shoulders. The fog horn grumbled its displeasure. A miserable, cold, wet summer afternoon and I get to visit The Bastard, he thought. Looks like the whole street is deserted. I've never seen fog this heavy before. Hope the bus will see me and stop. Shouldn't have any trouble finding a seat.

He didn't have to worry. The bus barely crawled down the street as it approached him, headlights trying to penetrate the gloom. It stopped, the doors creaked open, he boarded, sat near the front, and began his long, slow trip to the downtown area.

"Superior Street," the driver called out. Dave arose and stepped off. The bus slowly disappeared into the haze and left him standing alone. I've never seen this place so quiet, he thought, and shivered again from the moist, repressive air.

Brastad's Hardware was only a short distance from the bus stop and Dave quickened his pace to get there. Store signs were lit up, but couldn't be seen from any distance. Car traffic was absent. An occasional bus crept by. A pedestrian wearing a trench coat with turned-up collar stared at Dave as he passed. He probably wonders what the hell I'm doing out here, Dave thought. Well, so do I.

On reaching the hardware store, Dave opened the door and stepped inside. The store consisted of one cavernous room, not well lighted, and cluttered with paraphernalia from one end to the other. Shelves covered the walls and held dark objects of various sizes. Large, sinister gadgets dangled from the ceiling on ropes, grotesque stalactites in a creepy cave. There seemed to be no order to the disarray and Dave wondered how anything could ever be found. He looked around for help.

No one was there, no customers and no clerks. Glancing to the back of the store Dave noticed a door, slightly ajar, leading to a back room. He approached the door. "Mr. Brastad?" No answer. Again he called, "Mr. Brastad?" Still no answer. Gently he pushed open the door and eased inside the back room.

"Mr. Brastad?" Silence. Dave glanced around. A single bulb in the center of the ceiling provided the only illumination. Clutter formed dark levees around the base of the walls and a lone desk sat in the middle of the room. A side door provided access to the outside.

Dave approached the desk with curiosity. So this is where the old bastard works, eh. Order forms and receipts cluttered the top of the desk. A single drawer enticed Dave to open it.

Again he looked around. Again he called out, "Mr. Brastad?" Again no answer. He reached for the desk drawer and slowly drew it open.

The drawer contained several pencils, an eraser, some miscellaneous papers and a small object on a gold chain that glistened even in the dim light. Dave picked up the chain, watched the little pendant twirl about, and gasped. The ornament was a little gold airplane, a replica of a P-38, Mary Ann's plane.

At that instant the side door opened and The Bastard stepped in. He stared at Dave holding the airplane and began to shout, "What are you doing back here! Get out of my desk!" and he leaped across the room, lunging for the necklace.

Dave clutched the airplane in his fist, bounced backward, then veered to his left through the door to the main store. He raced past the clutter out into the fog and sped blindly back toward Lake Avenue and the Point.

He thought he saw The Bastard running after him and he was sure he heard the footsteps. In the fog, it was impossible to tell, so he kept on running, his breath now coming in gasps. Back to Lake Avenue. Down toward the bridge. Eventually, he had to stop and catch his breath.

Looking back, Dave strained his eyes, watching for any movement through the camouflaging fog. He momentarily stopped panting and listened for any faint sound. Was that a footstep? No time to wait and find out.

He turned and raced once more for the bridge just as it let loose with an ear-shattering blast that signaled an oncoming ship and increased his own panic. I've go to get there before the bridge goes up or I'll be trapped! and he forced his gasping body to continue.

The traffic arms were descending as Dave reached the bridge and scooted under. He continued his race across the bridge, but halfway to the other side felt the massive structure shudder as the span lifted from its moorings and began its ascent. By the time he reached the far side, the bridge was already twenty-five feet in the air and rising, too high to jump off.

Again he came to a stop, trying to regain his breath. Chances are, he thought, The Bastard didn't get on board the bridge so the best bet for me would be to go back to the middle, climb up to the operators house, and let the pilot know what's going on. He took two steps toward the center of the bridge when the sound of footsteps, slow but distinct, reached his ears and froze his blood. The Bastard must have made it!

Now what? Think, think! he told himself. Where could he hide? More footsteps, a little closer. Where can I go? He sped to the edge of the bridge, hesitated for a second, then crawled over the railing. Dangling down precariously from the side, he clutched a post, fingers interlocked the way Jake had advised. What if he spots me here?

He listened as the footsteps drew ever closer and at the same time a 600-foot ore boat broke through the fog as it entered the channel, its blazing lights fighting to penetrate the mist. The footsteps and the boat both approached Dave and the lights from the ship became a danger as they erased his cover of darkness. If he sees me, where can I go? Then he remembered.

During their examination of the bridge, Dave and Jake noticed angle beams running at forty-five degrees from the edge of the bridge to the main I-beams supporting the structure. One of those angle beams was within reach.

In the next few seconds, several events converged. The ore boat began passing directly below the bridge. The Bastard appeared, spotted Dave dangling from the post, and began to kick at his hands. Dave released one hand and grabbed an angled support beam with the other, then transferred his second hand to the beam and began a gradual slide under the bridge.

The Bastard saw his quarry escaping, and lunged over the railing. Too far. His violent movement left him teetering over the railing. He reached back for support but his hand slipped off the cold, wet metal. Dave watched as The Bastard pawed futilely, his hands clawing but grabbing only the damp air. The body toppled over the railing then continued on a strangely silent fall, twisting slightly, all the way to the deck of the ore boat, where it sprawled grotesquely, impaled on a belaying pin. A sailor on the ship ran to the body and stared in shock. He called out and several more men appeared. More yelling. Then, from the rear of the ship, a spotlight cut its way through the mist and swept across the risen bridge. Another voice, "There's somebody under that bridge!" Dave, who had worked his way to the top of the angle beam, locked his fingers together and clung ever tighter to his support.

The following thirty minutes blurred into a dream. The ore boat passed through the canal, the bridge came down, and the sound of men running on the metal sidewalk drew closer to the beam where Dave clung, body trembling. Bright lights shone down on him. A rope ladder appeared next to Dave and a husky, young man clambered down from the railing above. More ropes appeared, the husky man tied two ropes around Dave who, with some coaching, reluctantly released his grip from the beam and felt himself slowly pulled to safety atop the bridge. Several police cars sat on the bridge, their lights flashing. A doctor stepped up and gave the young adventurer a cursory examination. After being pronounced well, he got a short ride to a police station. Dave relinquished the tiny, golden airplane to the officers. A thousand questions followed. Finally, Carl and Tena Aune arrived and took their son home.

CHAPTER 19

Nazis Occupy Copenhagen

Duluth News Tribune, Summer, 1943

The next day, police and reporters descended on the Aune residence, all wanting to get the whole story. Dave's own folks had to know what happened, of course, but they acted more as protectors than inquisitors. Gradually the commotion abated.

The following days brought revelations. Police searched Brastad's house and discovered a dark room for developing pictures. Numerous photographs of Mary Ann, all of which appeared to be taken without her knowledge, hung from the walls of the room. Pictures of other young girls lay scattered throughout the residence. Boxes of pornographic magazines filled the closet of the bedroom. "It was shocking," said Police Chief Rubin.

The police released Buck Anderson and he and Jake appeared to be on good terms—at least for awhile. Birdy Gunderson continued to sing and whistle through his own special world. Scotty O'Doul worked on a new plan to expand his cellar without building a foundation. The city settled down, ore boats went on shuttling across the Great Lakes, and the unremitting war continued to send telegrams to grief-stricken families.

Dave and Jake began to plot their next escapade.

www.ingramcontent.com/pod-product-compliance
Lightning Source LLC
Chambersburg PA
CBHW032043180726
48284CB00008B/2726